LOOK AND FIND®

HAPPY FEET

Illustrated by Art Mawhinney

Published by Louis Weber, C.E.O., Publications International, Ltd.
7373 North Cicero Avenue, Lincolnwood, Illinois 60712

Ground Floor, 59 Gloucester Place, London W1U 8JJ

Customer Service: 1-800-595-8484 or
customer_service@pilbooks.com

www.pilbooks.com

Look and Find is a registered trademark of
Publications International, Ltd., in the United States and in Canada.

p i kids is a registered trademark of Publications International, Ltd.

8 7 6 5 4 3 2 1

ISBN-13: 978-1-4127-6492-6
ISBN-10: 1-4127-6492-0

publications international, ltd.

Penguins sing their special Heartsongs to find their true loves. Can you find Memphis and Norma Jean, who are together forever? Look for these other courting characters, too.

Memphis

Norma Jean

Miss Viola

Maurice

Noah

Eggbert

The baby penguins are here at last! Hatching from their eggs, the babies are shielded by their doting fathers. Look and find these little penguins who are new to the world.

Gloria

Seymour

Carl

Mike

Alan

Dennis

Brian

The young penguins aren't fuzzy any longer. They're not babies anymore, either! Look around the graduation party and find these celebrating penguins who are having a blast.

Mumble

Peachy

Flex

Frankie

Tab

Snow Doggie

Mumble's new homies take him to their cool Adelie 'hood. While they show off for some of the girls, can you find the ladies who laugh at the not-so-macho 'guins?

Coco

Lupe

Yolanda

Lola

Carmen

Rita

While swimming in an underwater cathedral of ice, Mumble and his Adelie pals discover a bizarre creature. Look around the excavator to find these human things scattered about.

Pencil

Work glove

Keys

Hula girl

Thermos

Snow goggles

Pop can

Mumble and the Amigos have come to Elephant Seal Land, where they are surrounded by these large, friendly creatures. Look for these not-so-small seals among the rest:

Pee Wee

Tom Thumb

Bitsy

Tiny

Teensy

Minnie

Lil

Smalls

Mumble is in the zoo — and his act is a hit! The crowd loves his tap-dancing. Look for these faces in the adoring crowd.

Professor Meredith Wilson

Mayor Penzance

Miss Folly Zeigfeld

Marian the Zoo's Librarian

Dr. Kelly Astaire

Rodgers Hart

Hammer Stein

At last Mumble has returned home to Antarctica and his fellow Emperor penguins. To celebrate, he taps out a very special dance routine. But he's not the only one dancing. Look for each of these other snazzy steps that are being performed.

Square-dancing

Can-can

Disco

Bunny hop

Hula

Tango

Hustle

Ballroom

These especially musical penguins are hidden in the Heartsong crowd. Can you find them?

Piccolo

Lullaby

Melody

Cello

Carol

Danny

Go back to the egg-hatching scene and count all of the unhatched eggs that you see. How many can you find?

Cowabunga! Splash back to the graduation shindig and see if you can spot partying penguins doing these different dives.

Cannonball

Parachute

Jackknife

Belly Flop

Can Opener

Swan Dive

File back into the Adelie Land and find these different rock formations among the penguins' rock piles:

Fence

Baseball Diamond

Pyramid

Stonehenge

Rock Garden

Totem Pole

Swim back to the underwater excavator and find these other human tools:

Ice ax

Ice screw

Sledgehammer

Ice drill

Ice saw

Shovel

Penguins aren't the only birds who live in Antarctica. Head back to Elephant Seal Land and find these other kinds of birds that live there:

Petrel

Tern

Skua

Albatross

Sheathbill

Cormorant

Gull

Fulmar

Tap your way back to the zoo and look for these snazzy souvenirs:

Penguin cap

A penguin coffee mug

A penguin t-shirt

Penguin doll

A book about penguins

A penguin beach towel

There are many other types of penguins in the world besides the Emperor, Adelie, and Rockhopper penguins that live in Antarctica. Return to the final dance scene and find these penguins that live all over the world.

Royal

Erect-crested

Humboldt

King

Fairy

African

Yellow-eyed

Galapagos